MOZART

Tonight

By

Julie Downing

BRADBURY PRESS
New York

Collier Macmillan Canada—Toronto
Maxwell Macmillan International Publishing Group
New York   Oxford   Singapore   Sydney

To Scott, who helps me keep everything in perspective

*The author would like to thank George Gelles,
executive director of the Philharmonia Baroque Orchestra,
for his thoughtful comments and generous help.*

*Bradbury Press
Macmillan Publishing Company
866 Third Avenue
New York, NY 10022*

*Collier Macmillan Canada, Inc.
1200 Eglinton Avenue East
Suite 200
Don Mills, Ontario M3C 3N1*

*First American edition
Printed and bound in Hong Kong by Toppan Printing Company
10   9   8   7   6   5   4   3   2
The text of this book is set in 13 point Palatino.
The illustrations are rendered in watercolor.
Book design by Julie Quan*

LIBRARY OF CONGRESS CATALOGING-IN-PUBLICATION DATA
Downing, Julie.
Mozart / by Julie Downing.
p.   cm.
Summary: On the eve of his great operatic triumph Don Giovanni.
Mozart looks back on the events of his life that led to this moment.
ISBN 0-02-732881-3
1. Mozart, Wolfgang Amadeus, 1756–1791—Juvenile literature.
2. Composers—Austria—Biography—Juvenile literature.   [1. Mozart,
Wolfgang Amadeus, 1756–1791.   2. Composers.]   I. Title.
ML3930.M9D68   1991
780'.92—dc20   [B]   90-34479

Wolfgang Amadeus Mozart, born January 27, 1756, was one of the greatest musical geniuses of all times. He began composing at the age of five, wrote his first symphony at the age of eight, and finished his first opera when he was twelve.

Mozart died at the age of thirty-six. He had composed over six hundred pieces in his lifetime.

Although Mozart was never financially successful, he had the courage to continue working in a time that did not always recognize his genius. His beautiful compositions are generally considered the greatest musical gift ever left by one man.

On the night of October 29, 1787, the opera house in Prague sparkled with thousands of candles. The composer Wolfgang Mozart was about to conduct his new opera, *Don Giovanni*. The merchants and their wives flocked to the galleries, and the poor begged for coppers to buy seats under the eaves. A line of coaches—fancy and plain—stretched all the way to the opera house entrance.

A rented coach rolled toward the theater. Inside, Wolfgang Mozart was peering out the window. He turned to his wife, Constanze, and said,

Stanzi, look at all the people! Everyone in Prague is coming to see my opera. I hope it is going to be a great success. If only Papa were alive to see the crowds. He would be so proud!

This is what Papa wanted for me from the moment I let out my first musical cry almost thirty-one years ago. He bundled me up and rushed me to the Salzburg Cathedral, where I was christened. I'm Joannes Chrysostumus Wolfgang Amadeus Mozart.

"Such a long name for such a little baby," laughed Mama. "I shall call him Wolfgang."

I loved growing up in Salzburg. Papa helped direct the Archbishop's orchestra, and our house was always filled with music.

I listened when Papa gave my sister, Nannerl, her piano lessons. She told me I wrote musical notes before I could write words.

When I was six, Papa gave me my first violin. I begged and begged to play with him.

"Wolfi, you don't know how to play the violin yet," scolded Papa. "When you are older I will give you lessons. But now, let my friends and me practice in peace."

"Don't cry, Wolfi." Herr Schachtner lifted me onto a chair next to him.

"Let the boy try, Leopold. He can play softly. You will never hear him."

I played very quietly. After only a few bars, Herr Schachtner put down his violin and let me play alone. Papa listened, too. I think he hardly saw the notes in front of him. His eyes were full of tears.

The next day Papa started my lessons. I learned to play both the piano and the violin!

"My son," Papa said, "if you work very hard, when
you grow up, the Emperor will offer you a position as court
musician. But first, people must hear great things about
Wolfgang Mozart."

Mama, Papa, Nannerl, and I packed our best clothes,
tied my clavichord to the roof of a coach, and left Salzburg.
My sister and I gave concerts in many cities and soon
arrived in Vienna. The Empress of Austria loved our music!
We stayed in the capital for over a month and played for
her family and friends. Papa often let my sister and me stay
up long past our bedtime. Once, we played duets until two
A.M. Then a carriage rushed us to a huge house, where we
played until dawn.

"Bravo, little Mozart!" The Count clapped loudly. He pressed a pair of shoe buckles into Papa's hand. "You must accept this generous gift in payment for your children's concert."

"How am I supposed to pay our bills with these?" muttered Papa. But he never asked for more, only bowed and humbly accepted the buckles.

I grew up on the sound of our coach wheels as they clattered over streets. Papa took us through France, Germany, and Italy. We even played for the King of England.

Sometimes Papa and I traveled alone, but I liked it best when Mama and Nannerl came, too.

The year I turned sixteen, the Archbishop of Salzburg died, and the new Archbishop demanded that I enter his service.

In the spring of 1781, I took a trip to Vienna with the Archbishop. As always, I was treated like a servant. I ate with the cooks and stood behind the footmen. I was allowed to play only when the Archbishop ordered, and then only what he wanted to hear.

I had to sneak out of the palace at night to practice my own music. Often, I played all night, and returned to my room just as the sun was rising.

One morning I was tiptoeing back to my room when a voice boomed, "Mozart!" I turned to face the Archbishop. He said, "You know I have forbidden all my servants to play on their own. You have not followed my wishes. You will learn your place! I command you to return to Salzburg."

"I know your grace is not pleased with me. Why send me to Salzburg? Why not just dismiss me?"

"Scoundrel! Vagabond!" The Archbishop's nose turned purple. "You dare to threaten me! I want nothing more to do with you!"

I took a deep breath. "Nor I with you! Tomorrow you shall have my resignation in writing." And with that, I turned and stomped out of the room.

The door slammed shut behind me with a bang.
Vienna spread out before me. I thought, this is the city of
art and music. Vienna will be my home!

Do you remember our first home together, Stanzi? Just four tiny rooms, overlooking the market square. I can still hear the fat Count puffing up all those stairs for his piano lessons. Each morning I woke to the bells of St. Stephen's chiming six o'clock. I heard the steady *clop, clop, clop* of the farmers' carts coming to market.

"Fish for sale," sang the fishmonger. "Fresh fish today."

"Buy my pears," called the fruit seller. "Ripe oranges and lemons."

Roosters crowed, children laughed, and maids gossiped by the fountain. I listened as a chorus of voices rang through the street, and my mind filled with music.

❧

We were so happy. At last I was free to write any music I wanted. The street noise, memories of a carnival, or our babies' cries would spark a bit of music. I wrote furiously, scribbling notes on any scrap of paper I could find.

Each evening people crowded to my
concerts. Counts and countesses sent us stacks of
invitations. Everyone wanted to be the first to
hear my latest sonata.

I know you haven't forgotten the stacks of
bills. The copiest, the ushers, and the musicians
wanted money. There was a bill for the rent, and
a bill for the candles to light the concert hall. By
the time everyone else had been paid, there were
only a few ducats left for us.

If only the Emperor would offer me a court position. I began composing music for a new opera, *The Marriage of Figaro*. The story is about a servant who plays a trick on his master. The Emperor thought this was a very bad idea for an opera.

"But Your Majesty," I said, "the public is tired of stories about Greek gods. My opera is about ordinary people. Figaro is just a man."

Finally, the Emperor allowed me to perform the opera at the court theater. You and I, Constanze, danced with joy.

Many people tried to stop my opera, but in May 1786, *The Marriage of Figaro* opened. I raised my baton and the opera began. My enemies were not happy, but opening night, the audience cheered, and the Emperor yelled, "Bravo, Mozart!"

"A very good effort, Mozart," the Emperor said. "But you ask too much of the public. An opera should never last more than three hours, and *The Marriage of Figaro* went on longer. Court Composer Salieri's opera is shorter. That is much better."

My opera closed after only nine performances, and I still did not have a court position.

All winter creditors banged on our front door.

"Where is the rent money, Herr Mozart?"

"Pay me for your new coat."

"You owe me for your wife's medicine."

I hardly heard their cries; my mind was filled with music.

Spring finally arrived, and with it, good news from nearby Prague. It seemed the capital city had gone mad for *The Marriage of Figaro*. People hummed the tunes and danced to the music. They wanted more. I was invited to their city to write a new opera.

It is hard to believe that it was only six months ago that I started to write the music for *Don Giovanni*. My dear Constanze, you have had such patience for the last two weeks while we rehearsed the opera.

I know Herr Bondini, the manager of the opera, was not pleased to see me at last night's party.

"Mozart, I am glad you are enjoying yourself," he said. "But *Don Giovanni* opens tomorrow, and no one has seen the overture."

I danced a jig. "Don't worry, mein Herr, it's done."

Bondini grabbed me and led me to the piano, but I waved him away. "No, no, I don't need that. I always compose here." I tapped my forehead. "I hear the music in my mind. Now I just have to write it down, and that is very boring."

The singing and dancing amused me while I wrote. You, dear wife, stayed up long after the last guest had gone home. You kept me awake with your best fairy stories. By five o'clock this morning the overture was finished.

Suddenly the Mozarts' carriage stopped at the theater
door. Wolfgang and Constanze looked out the window.

"We're here at last!"

Wolfgang helped his wife out of the coach. As Constanze
took his arm, she thought, Wolfi, you have worked
so hard on this opera. I hope people love it.

They stepped into the theater just as the musicians
filed into their places. Mozart waited behind the stage door
while the overture, still wet with ink, was passed around.
As Mozart stepped through the door, he whispered to
himself, "My opera must be a success."

The musicians were ready. The audience waited. Mozart bowed, winked at Constanze, and picked up his baton.

A heavy chord broke the silence. Then another. The woodwinds burst in like a crowd in the marketplace, followed by a rush of violins. The music was dark and bright at the same time.

The orchestra paused and the curtain rose on *Don Giovanni*. The singers sang as they never had before. Mozart's music filled the opera house.

The final curtain came down. The theater was silent.
Then, the audience broke into wild applause. From the
boxes, the noblemen yelled, "Bravo, Mozart!" The towns-
people stamped their feet, and the violinists beat their bows
against their instruments. Constanze's heart filled with pride.

Wolfgang Mozart was raised onto the stage. He stared
at the cheering crowd. Then he stepped forward, stretched
out his hands, and took a deep bow.

A Note from the Author

I do not remember the first time I heard Wolfgang Mozart's music. It seems that I have always been aware of the composer and enjoyed the sparkle and life that characterize his music. In 1986, my husband and I spent Christmas in Vienna. I was overwhelmed by the beauty of the city. Vienna seemed to glow with the elegance of the eighteenth century, and I loved the history that surrounded me. I also felt the quiet presence of Mozart in many of the places we visited. We toured Schönbrunn Palace and saw the hall where he and Nannerl performed for the Empress and her family. I stood in the room where Mozart composed *The Marriage of Figaro* and listened to his music in St. Stephen's, the same cathedral where he and Constanze were married. This visit to Vienna brought Mozart to life.

I took another trip to Austria in February 1988. This trip was to focus on Mozart and his family. We visited small towns in the Alps, where I sketched rural life and gained a sense of the Mozarts' travels. Next we went to Salzburg, a city that has changed little since Mozart's time. The house where he was born remains in the old city, and the cathedral where he was baptized still dominates the cityscape. The baby was actually baptized Joannes Chrysostomus Wolgangus Theophilus Mozart. Wolfgang, however, preferred the Latin form of Theophilus, which is Amadeus. He referred to himself as Wolfgang Amadeus Mozart.

Our final stop was Vienna. This city has changed a great deal. Many eighteenth-century buildings were lost during the war, but the feeling of light, color, and grandeur remain the same. I relied on paintings and prints from the Museen der Stadt and the Belvedere Palace to give me an overview of eighteenth-century Viennese architecture, and photographed smaller details on some of the buildings. I studied many paintings and books to learn about the clothes people wore and the rooms they lived in. I was always interested in discovering as many details about ordinary life as I could. A late seventeenth-century painting showed a backgammon board on the floor. I realized Mozart, who loved games of strategy, might have played. I looked at paintings that showed marketplaces, doctors and their patients, and families eating breakfast. All these images helped me to imagine Vienna in the eighteenth century.

The Victoria and Albert Museum in London and the Metropolitan Museum in New York were invaluable sources for costumes and musical instruments from the period. The clavichord was an early keyboard instrument. Travelers often used a clavichord because it was small and easy to carry; Mozart's was tied to the roof of his coach. The instrument Mozart is playing on the cover is a pianoforte, which became popular in the 1770s. The pianoforte has fewer keys, but is more like our modern piano in that it can be played loudly or softly. *Piano e forte* is Italian and means "soft and loud."

Several books, including *Mozart* by Hugh Ottaway, *Mozart the Man—The Musician* by Arthur Hutchings, and *Mozart, The Golden Years* by H. C. Robbins Landon, were excellent sources for images and facts about the composer. The best sources of information were the actual letters of the Mozart family. These letters give a sense of the composer and important events, as well as a view into everyday life and Wolfgang's relationships with the people around him.

I chose to fictionalize some scenes in order to bring Mozart and his time to life. However, the details and dialogue of these scenes are based on letters written by and about the Mozart family. The dialogue in the scene between the Archbishop and Mozart was taken from a letter written by Wolfgang to his father on May 9, 1781. The letter details the outburst, and also provides insight into the position of a musician in the eighteenth century. Mozart was considered just a servant. In a letter dated March 17, 1781, Mozart grumbled to his father, "The two valets sit at the head of the table, but I have the honor at least of sitting above the cooks." Wolfgang was outraged by his treatment, and it was this sense of injustice and his independent spirit that gave him the courage to break with the Archbishop.

The letters also gave me an insight into the way Mozart composed his music. The creative process is a very personal form of expression and is difficult to understand, particularly in the case of a genius like Mozart. Even Wolfgang admitted that he was not always sure where his ideas came from. In one letter he wrote, "When I am, as it were, completely by myself and entirely alone and of good cheer, say traveling in a carriage, or walking after a good meal, or during the night when I cannot sleep…my ideas flow best and abundantly. Whence and how they came I know not, nor can I force them. Those ideas that please me I retain in memory, and am accustomed, as I have been told, to hum them to myself."

I do not know for sure if Mozart collected bits and pieces of music on his walk through the market square, but this letter, together with my impressions of the sounds that probably surrounded Mozart, prompted me to write the scene about the marketplace.

The letter continues to describe the actual writing of his music. Wolfgang rarely made rough drafts. Instead, the music seemed to pour out of his head in a completely finished form, as depicted in the scene which took place the night before *Don Giovanni* opened. Some people think the overture was written two days before the premiere. However, whether the music was written one day or two days before the opera opened, the story does show Mozart's ability to compose in his mind.

Many fellow musicians, including Emperor Joseph's Court Composer Antonio Salieri, were very jealous of the seemingly effortless way Mozart composed. Salieri recognized Wolfgang's talent and did all he could to stop his advancement. Rumors of sabotage by Salieri surrounded the opening of *The Marriage of Figaro*. Leopold wrote to Nannerl in April 1786 that he hoped the opera would succeed, "…for I know there are astonishingly strong cabals against it. Salieri and all his partisans will move heaven and earth." Salieri supposedly tried to pay off the singers and musicians to ruin the opera, but fortunately the plot did not succeed. *The Marriage of Figaro* was a great success that evening. Mozart received so many requests for encores that the opera lasted into the early morning. This prompted Emperor Joseph to issue an order that no piece of music should be encored.

Mozart received about two hundred dollars for his score, and never another penny. It closed after nine performances, although it was revived for twenty-six others in 1789–90. At the time, few people had the remotest idea that *Figaro* was a classic.

Mozart's letters also provided inspiration for specific details in the illustrations. Before Wolfgang and Constanze were married, Constanze received an angry letter from Mozart. He was outraged when, at a party, she allowed another man to measure her leg with a ribbon. This was a popular and risqué party game, and although Mozart did not disapprove of the game, he did not think it was appropriate for his fiancée. This is the game that is illustrated in the party scene before *Don Giovanni* opened. Today, this game seems very innocent, and the letter is another clue to the time in which Mozart lived.

Throughout my research and writing of *Mozart Tonight*, I was constantly trying to understand Mozart as well as the time in which he lived. During the process, I marveled at Mozart's talent and courage. He was at times vain and frivolous, and like most people in the eighteenth century, very concerned with appearances. During the nine years he and his family lived in Vienna, they moved twelve times. Mozart never seemed to have quite enough money to pay the rent. And yet, the family usually had servants, Wolfgang loved clothes, and he and Constanze gave many parties. They did charge the men who attended, but still spent far more than they could afford. He was sentimental and childlike. When his pet starling died, during the writing of *Don Giovanni*, he held an elaborate funeral and composed music in memory of the bird.

As a composer, he enjoyed some great success, and yet died penniless. Musical tastes changed, and the Viennese were a fickle audience. As early as 1782, the Emperor, after a production of Mozart's *The Abduction from the Seraglio*, complained that his music had too many notes, and he should just cut a few.

Today, we recognize Mozart as one of the finest and most versatile composers. His music soars with hope and optimism. Mozart, through the creations of his mind and spirit, has truly become immortal.

—*Julie Downing*
San Francisco, 1990